NHA

DISCARD

For Michelle

A Doubleday Book for Young Readers

Published by Delacorte Press
Bantam Doubleday Dell Publishing Group, Inc.
1540 Broadway, New York, New York 10036

Doubleday and the portrayal of an anchor with a dolphin
are trademarks of Bantam Doubleday Dell Publishing Group, Inc.

© John Rowe 1996
First American edition 1996
Originally published in the United Kingdom in 1996 by Hutchinson Children's Books

Library of Congress Cataloging-in-Publication Data
Rowe, John.
Can you spot the spotted dog? / John Rowe.—1st ed.
p.   cm.
"Originally published in the United Kingdom in 1996 by Hutchinson Children's Books"—T.p. verso.
Summary: The reader is asked to find a growing list of animals in the accompanying illustrations before going on to the next page.
ISBN 0-385-32207-0 (alk. paper)
[1. Animals—Fiction.   2. Picture puzzles.]   I. Title.
PZ7.F8345Can   1996
[E]—dc20   95-26630   CIP   AC

The text of this book is set in Palatino Light.
Manufactured in Hong Kong

October 1996
1 3 5 7 9 10 8 6 4 2

Can You Spot the Spotted Dog?

John Rowe

A Doubleday Book for Young Readers

Can you spot the spotted dog?

If you can, turn the page.

Can you spot the spotted dog
And the little white owl?

If you can, turn the page.

Can you spot the spotted dog
And the little white owl
And the jet black cat?

If you can, turn the page.

Can you spot the spotted dog
And the little white owl
And the jet black cat
And the tiny gray mouse?

If you can, turn the page.

Can you spot the spotted dog
And the little white owl
And the jet black cat
And the tiny gray mouse
And the slippery snake?

If you can, turn the page.

Can you spot the spotted dog

And the little white owl

And the jet black cat

And the tiny gray mouse

And the slippery snake

And the furry mole?

If you can, turn the page.

Can you spot the spotted dog
And the little white owl
And the jet black cat
And the tiny gray mouse
And the slippery snake
And the furry mole
And the prickly hedgehog?

If you can, turn the page.

Can you spot the spotted dog
And the little white owl
And the jet black cat
And the tiny gray mouse
And the slippery snake
And the furry mole
And the prickly hedgehog
And the bright white butterfly?

If you can, turn the page.

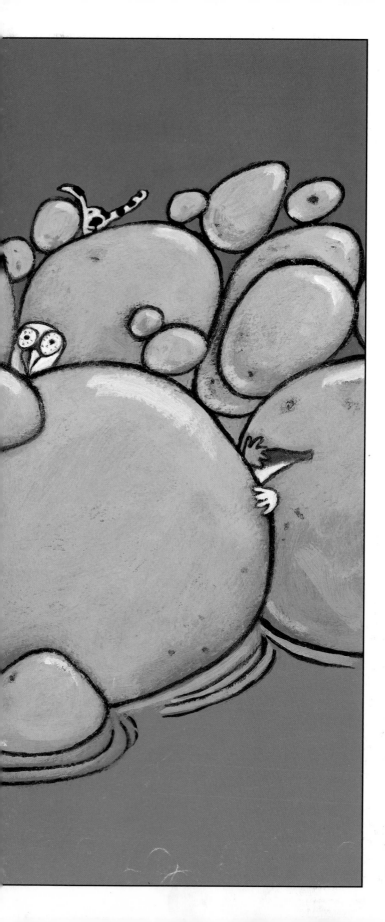

Can you spot the spotted dog
And the little white owl
And the jet black cat
And the tiny gray mouse
And the slippery snake
And the furry mole
And the prickly hedgehog
And the bright white butterfly
And the hungry hippo?

If you can, turn the page.

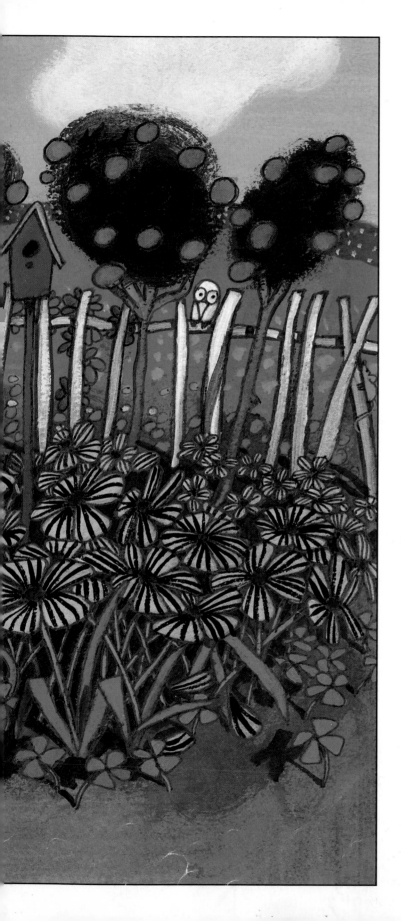

Can you spot the spotted dog

And the little white owl

And the jet black cat

And the tiny gray mouse

And the slippery snake

And the furry mole

And the prickly hedgehog

And the bright white butterfly

And the hungry hippo

And the busy bee?

If you can, turn the page.

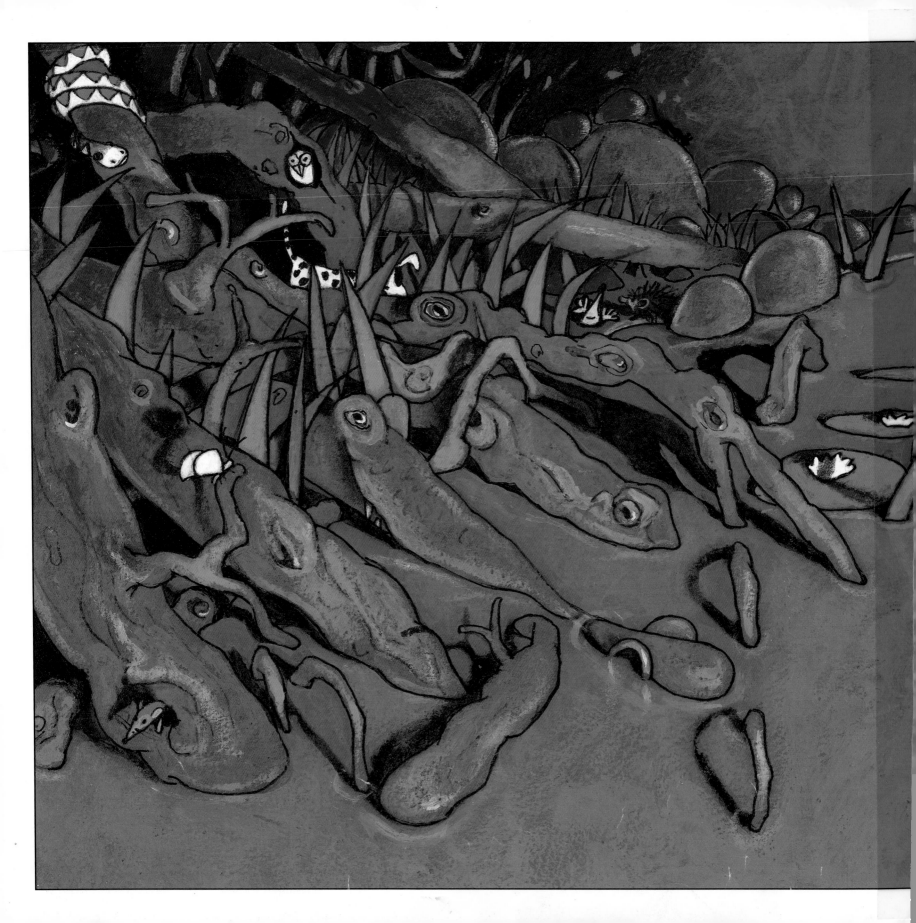

Can you spot the spotted dog

And the little white owl

And the jet black cat

And the tiny gray mouse

And the slippery snake

And the furry mole

And the prickly hedgehog

And the bright white butterfly

And the hungry hippo

And the busy bee

And the long green crocodile?

If you can, turn the page.

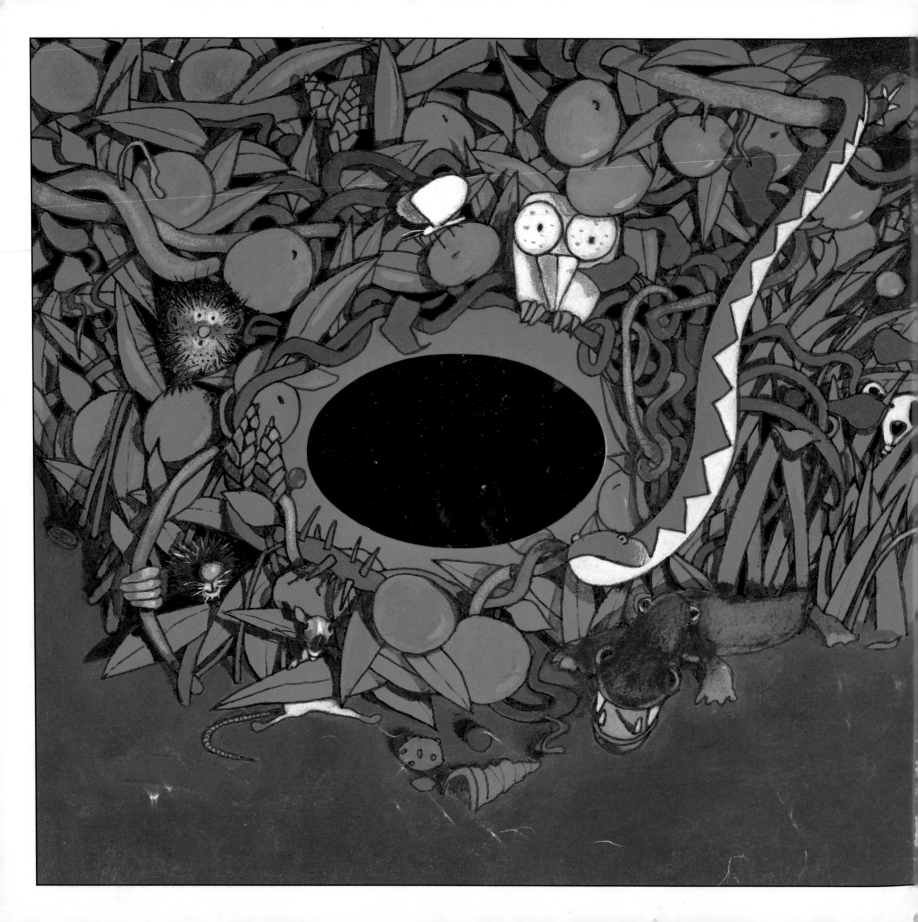

Can you spot the spotted dog

And the little white owl

And the jet black cat

And the tiny gray mouse

And the slippery snake

And the furry mole

And the prickly hedgehog

And the bright white butterfly

And the hungry hippo

And the busy bee

And the long green crocodile?

And who is the little rascal
in the middle?